Sex, S

C000126767

Mistletoe

Laura Barnard

Jeanette,

I hope you have a fabulous Christmas!

Love + laughs
Laura Barnard
6   6   ⨯

Sex, Snow and Mistletoe

Snow, bloody snow! The only idiots that like snow are kids and that's because they get a day off school. It's us adults that have to carry on like normal and suffer. Like I'm not late enough. Like I'm not already two hours late for the rehearsal dinner. Gabriella is going to kill me. She's text me fifteen times already and left three furious voice mails. I've ignored them all, refusing to answer the phone while I'm driving. I'd no doubt crash the car and that would only make me later. It's not my fault that my boss kept me late at work and then my Mum popped round and started blabbering on about how I should be going to my own wedding, not a friend of a friends.

To be honest I'm quite embarrassed to have even been invited to this. I've only met her once. I mean, do people really invite people to their wedding that they met when urinating in the street? I don't really think I was proving my wedding guest potential, more my inability to drink three bottles of wine and remain standing/coherent/able to hold my bladder.

Lights suddenly flash in my rear mirror. I glance back and notice a black Audi behind me. I look out of the window past the blizzard of snow falling onto the already dark muddy country lane, big willow trees surrounding me. This is definitely the kind of place people get murdered. There is no way in hell I'm pulling over so this psychopath can pull a gun on me. No thank you. I watch Crime Watch. My mumma didn't raise no fool. I check the lights on my dashboard, wondering if there's something obvious I'm missing. I think I'm fine... Not that I'd have the slightest idea anyway. I hate being such a girl.

My phone starts ringing again. I can just imagine Gabriella now, crouched over her phone in a corner, fuming at being there on her own. Maybe I should answer it, get the drama over and done with. I scramble in my bag and pick up the phone.

"Where the fuck are you?" she screams before I've even had a chance to say hello. Never one to hold back is our Gabriella.

"Babe I'm just on my way, I promise."

"You promise?" she shouts. "You promised two fucking hours ago! Where the hell are you? Do you have any idea how embarrassing this is for me? Everyone keeps asking me why I'm here alone. I would have dragged along some dickhead man if I'd have known you were going to stand me up!"

Jesus, she's really raging. She must be on the champagne, she always gets extra crazy on champagne. She once punched me in the face because I ate the last malteaser. I was out cold for three hours.

Lights flash in my mirror again. Why won't this guy leave me alone? I look in the mirror trying to work out what he's trying to tell me. He flashes his lights a few more times and for a second they dazzle me, making me only able to see white light. I open my eyes to see purple and blue spots float around me. I blink, desperate to clear them just in time to see the tree I'm about to smack into. I slam the brakes on and clamp my eyes shut as I skid into it.

I'm going to die! I'm going to die! I just know it.

The air bag smacks me in the face, almost suffocating me. A loud crunching sound goes crashing through my ears and then my engine squeals like an injured animal. I open my eyes and look around me, pushing the airbag out of the way.

Am I alive? Is this heaven? Am I going to go into heaven like Patrick Swayze in Ghost? Or is this hell, forever being forced to live my own pathetic life?

I look out of the windscreen to find I'm not facing a tree. I crane my neck to see that the back end of the car crashed into the tree and thankfully it's not a head on collision. I feel around my body and for some miraculous reason I seem to be completely unharmed. Unfortunately I can't say the same about my car.

"Are you okay?" a voice asks, opening my door.

A vision in his early thirties with impeccably groomed hair the colour of dark chocolate is looking over me concerned. Wowzas.

"Erm...yeah, I'm fine thanks." I smile politely, wondering who this gorgeous stranger is.

This gorgeous stranger that did in fact cause me to crash. The maniac could have killed me. But... He's so pretty.

"I tried to flash you; you had smoke coming out of your exhaust pipe," he explains, flashing me a beautiful toothy grin.

"Really?" I ask completely baffled. I can't seem to concentrate on anything but the way his lips pout.

"Yeah," he smiles with concern around his eyes. His

stunning emerald eyes. They almost look too unusual to be real. Maybe contacts? "Do you want me to call the AA for you?"

"Um...no." My head is still swimming. Concentrate Mel. "I need to get to a wedding. I'm already late and my friend's going to kill me."

"Really?" He smiles strangely. "What wedding?"

I look at him, trying to work out if I've seen him on Crime Watch before. If he's the kind of man that follows women on dark country roads and flashes their lights until they crash and then strangles them to death. His arms in that tight t-shirt do look strong enough. *Mmm, yeah they do.* But why is he wearing a t-shirt in this weather? Another sign he could be a psychopath.

"I'm not sure I should tell you," I grumble cautiously.

He smiles, revealing perfect cheek dimples. "Well, you're obviously from the bride's side. How do you know Olivia?"

Oh thank God.

"You're going to the same wedding?" I ask in surprise. He's not a killer! Yay.

"Yep and I can give you a lift if you want."

I let myself relax for second. I'm going to get there on

time and Gabriella's going to calm the hell down.

He helps me out of the car, checking that I haven't got any injuries even though I insist I don't and then carries my luggage into his car. I'm a little embarrassed when he sees I brought three cases, but I mean, you never know how much you're gonna need!

"So, seriously," he asks as we drive along, "how do you know Olivia?"

Flashes of that night come into my head. God, the horror.

"Oh, she's more a friend of a friend. I've only really met her once," I answer vaguely. I look out of the window at the growing snow storm, hoping he doesn't press me for information.

"And what did you think of her?"

Damn it. I turn to face him to see his forehead creased in concentration.

I think back to that night. Olivia is a petite, blonde woman shaped a bit like a fairy. Her personality however, isn't so pretty. I mean, fair enough I was peeing in the street, but I do think she was pretty judgemental. She probably only invited me to laugh at but Gabriella went to school with her and won't have a word said against her.

8

"Honestly?" I ask testing the water.

He smiles back. "Yep."

I sigh, resigned to telling him the truth. I might as well. "I thought she was a stuck up cow," I eventually confess. I squirm uncomfortably in my chair waiting for his reaction.

After a slight pause he bursts out laughing making me jump with fright. He's laughing so hard I think *he* might wet himself.

"What? You said to be honest!" I fold my arms defensively over my chest, feeling exposed. He's probably her best friend or something. I knew I shouldn't have said anything.

"And honest you were," he smiles back, his eyes creased with confusion.

I smile too realising that he is quite exceptionally good looking. His eyes are such an unusual clear green and they really stand out against his dark hair. He could be a bloody model. Maybe he is.

"So do you like her?" I ask, desperate to break the awkward silence.

"Oh yeah, of course." He smiles weakly. *"Well..."*

"Well?" I encourage. I knew it. He hates her too.

He avoids my gaze, looking at the road. "I mean,

9

sometimes I love her and then other times I can't stand the girl."

"Wow," I whisper taken aback. "You sound like you know her pretty well. I almost feel bad for slating her." Only almost. She's a bitch.

"Yeah, I'm actually involved in the wedding."

Shit. I've only gone and slagged her off to a bloody usher. He's probably one of the groom's best friends. Idiot, *idiot*.

"Wow, you're pretty late aren't you?" I laugh trying to quickly lighten the mood.

A streetlight flashes over him, lighting up the devilish glint in his eyes. "Yep, that's me, always late."

"That's weird, that's what my friends say about me." I think of all of the times I've been told off because of it. They've said I'll be late for my own funeral.

"Well maybe we've got loads in common. They say sometimes you can find your new best friend in the weirdest places." He wiggles his eyebrows suggestively at me.

I look back at him, trying to work out if he's flirting with me. If he is that might be the worst chat up line I've ever heard, but instead of being horrified I find myself suppressing a giggle. He smiles back. Thank God he's taking the piss.

"Okay then, Mr New Best Friend," I joke, sitting up straighter in my chair, "let's give you a bit of a quiz to see just how compatible we are."

"Shoot," he replies with an easy smile, turning down the radio.

"Okay, dogs or cats?"

"Dogs," he answers immediately. Good choice.

"Jam or marmalade?"

"Jam."

"Pizza or garlic bread?"

He grins back at me. "Both, with ketchup."

Wow, this is kind of freaky. He's like a male version of me.

"Pippa or Kate?"

"Camilla," he replies raising his eyebrows up and down comically.

I burst out laughing. "*Oooh,* controversial."

So far he's working out to be my perfect man. Well, apart from that whole Camilla thing which I'm taking as a joke.

"Forgive or revenge?"

"Easy, forgive. God," he exhales sharply, "these

11

questions really are boring. Can't you think of any better ones?"

"Um..."

He rolls his eyes at my obvious lack of imagination. "Okay, my turn. If you had to kill a member of your family, who would it be?"

"Fuck! What?" I stutter.

He bursts out laughing. It's such a beautiful sound.

"I'm only joking, but come on. I'm sure you've got an Aunt or something that you wouldn't miss."

I begrudgingly chuckle. "I don't know. I think I'd miss them all."

He takes his eyes off the road for a second and then meets mine. He's so breathtakingly beautiful that I've suddenly forgotten how to breathe. How do I do it again? That's right, in and out.

Suddenly I'm thrown forward in my seat and then back just as harsh. Fuck, my neck kills. I look around to see him trying to control the wheel. What the hell is happening? The car chugs, causing it to skid slightly from side to side. I'm going to be sick. Please God, save me. I'm too young and pretty to die.

It finally slows and then comes to a total stop on the side

of the road.

"What the hell was that?" I gasp, completely out of breath from another near death experience. Two in one night. That's got to be some kind of record.

His face curls up in bewilderment, adorable wrinkles forming around his eyes. "I have no fucking idea." He starts looking at the lights on the dashboard. "I'm gonna check under the hood."

I look out of the window. The snow is pelting down now and he's only wearing that flimsy t-shirt and jeans. "In this weather? Are you insane?"

He grabs a quilted duffle coat from the back seat and jumps out of the car, pulling the hood up. I jump out too, wrapping my burgundy parka coat tighter around me. It's so cold out here I can see my own breath. I look along the long, dark country lane quickly filling up with thick white snow. *So* not the ideal place to break down.

I go to join him looking at the engine. He's looking really hard at it but not actually doing anything. I stand really close to him, desperate for any kind of heat from his body.

"So..." I eventually say. "What are you looking at here?"

He looks up at me, biting his lip. "If I'm honest, I have no fucking idea."

I frown in confusion. He has to be joking right?

"I know. I'm a guy and I have no idea about cars. I was really planning on just calling the AA or something but I haven't got any service."

Shit. I've broken down with the one male species who knows fuck all about cars.

"So what are we going to do?"

He shrugs, wrapping his coat tighter round his neck. "Can I suggest we continue this conversation in the car? With the heating on?"

We get in, slamming the doors after us and turn the heating on full. I rub my hands together trying to put some feeling back in them. It's bloody freezing out there. I put my hands over the heaters, feeling I need to thaw out. I know I'm hogging the heat, but I really don't care right now.

"So... I don't want to sound like a nag and all, but...what do you plan to do?"

He looks at his phone again frowning heavily, then looks out at the increasing blizzard and night sky.

"Well... My phone doesn't have any service and it's pitch black outside. I can't see any street lights and the snows coming down pretty heavy."

Well he's good at stating the obvious. Wait, did I even

bring my phone with me after I crashed? I empty the contents of my handbag but can't find it. Damn

"Riiiiiight....?" I press.

"So I think our best plan would be to sleep in here tonight and then set off walking in the morning."

The Morning? Is he *insane?*

"But the wedding is tomorrow. Isn't that cutting it bloody fine?" Just imagining Gabriella's fury is enough to give me a headache.

He smiles. "Yeah. We'll miss the rehearsal dinner tonight, but to be honest I don't think we have much other choice. We could get lynched by wolves or something."

Wolves? I crease over in laughter. "Who knew you were a drama queen! That's so funny!"

"You don't know what the hells out there!" he retorts.

I laugh again. He really is too funny.

"Anyway, let's pass some time," he suggests, moving my hands off the heater so he can get some heat. "I think it was my turn for questions. What was your childhood like?"

"Woah," I gasp, blinking widely. "Straight to the personal questions! You haven't even asked my name!"

He grins mischievously. "Why waste time? This way I get to find out straight away if you have a crazy family. A name doesn't tell me anything."

"I can tell you straight away that I do." I think of my Mum. God, how do I put her? He looks at me expectantly. "Well…My childhood was fine. I'm an only child, but I always remember having loads of fun with my mum and Dad. Anyway, when I was eighteen my Dad left my Mum for another woman. She's never really gotten over it and, well, she kind of leans on me a lot."

"So she's a bit of a nightmare?" he asks seriously.

I smile to myself. "You're good at reading between the lines." I shake my head, desperate to change the subject. "Anyway, my turn."

"You really don't like personal questions do you?" he grins.

I ignore him. "What is your name anyway?"

"Lets not do names. Names give us a preconception of who we are. Until we get to the wedding lets just call each other Guy and Girl, okay?"

Wow, this brother's deep. Sexy, funny *and* deep. I hit the jackpot. I don't care if his names IP Freely. I want him.

"Okay," I say cautiously. "Lets do another question. Now this one will really tell me a lot about you. What's your favourite bit about a wedding?"

"Easy," he grins. "It's the end of the night when they're playing the last few songs. Everyone's really drunk by this point so everyone's dancing like they never want the music to stop. I like to look around at people. The Bride and Groom always look so happy, so glad that the day has gone without a hitch and everyone else is just so euphoric. You're surrounded by your friends and family and it's one of those rare moments where you can really feel the love in the room and think this is what life's all about."

Oh my God. He's my ideal man. No man has ever seemed sexier to me. That's what I always say. No-one's ever had the same answer as me before.

"Wow, that's the same moment as me!" I giggle gleefully, barely able to contain myself. I could really lower myself on his lap and gyrate like a stripper now. "That's so weird."

"Yeah right," he smirks, rolling his eyes. "You're just taking the piss now."

He thinks I'm mocking him? Oh my God, this guy is too good to be true.

"No, I swear! Most people say when the groom sees the bride for the first time. You can ask Gabriella when you meet her."

Shit, Gabriella. She really is going to kill me. Oh well.

I look at him wondering what his name is. My eyes travel of their own accord down his body. I bet he's buff as hell. All angled muscles. Ooh, maybe he has tattoos. Just seeing his forearms earlier tells me I'm right. Sexy forearms say a lot about a person. Gabriella's always agreed with me there.

A thrill of excitement shoots through my veins at the idea of seeing him naked. I'd probably pass out from pure shock.

"What's wrong?" he asks, concern creasing his features. His beautiful bloody features.

"Nothing," I shrug, dropping my eyes to the floor in a flush of embarrassment. I hope it's not obvious on my face what I was thinking. "I was just thinking that Gabriella will be worried."

He licks his lips, staring at me with a sudden intensity I've never seen before. He's not smiling at me anymore. He's looking at me with hunger in those hypnotising green eyes. I find myself staring at his plump pink lips. My stomach stirs with anticipation. It's been silent too long now. We're both just staring at each other, both our chests heaving erratically up and down.

I really want him to kiss me. I'm so conscious of being alone with him in this confined space. It's like sparks of electricity are bouncing off us towards each other.

He places his palm around my chin, his touch burning. I shamelessly lean into it welcoming his touch. His thumb grazes over my lips. A small moan escapes from them. How embarrassing. I sound totally wanton.

Slowly, painfully slowly, he leans forward, his hand slipping into my hair. His lips touch mine tentatively, barely a peck, before pausing and locking eyes with me. As if asking permission to continue. I push my lips onto his greedily. Both of his hands lock onto the back of my neck, his kisses becoming more urgent.

I gasp, desperate to allow in some breath and he takes the chance to tease his tongue into my mouth. Its patient, yet urgent. I can feel him holding himself back, trying to be a gentleman. Fuck that. I want more.

Before I have time to talk myself out of it I've crawled and positioned myself straddled over his lap. I grip onto his hair, pulling at the strands almost in anger that he's being such a gentleman. I want him to take control and throw me around. Who knew I was such a harlot! I don't even know this guy's name!

I reach down and wrap my fingers around his erection through his jeans. Wow, someone's a big boy! I position myself over it and rock, grinding so I can get the perfect friction. An almost pained growl escapes his lips.

He pulls my long hair to one side, tugging my coat off. I shrug it off, helping to shed me of my suddenly suffocating clothes. He grips the bottom of my jumper locking his eyes with me again, but this time those green eyes are alight with lust. A tingle of excitement runs from my throat to the pit of my stomach. In one firm sweep the jumper is pulled over my head. The static makes my hair wild which from the throbbing erection beneath me, he seems to like.

Normally I'd feel self-conscious the first time I stand in just my bra in front of a guy, but the way his eyes rake over me like I'm some precious jewel he's just discovered; well, it gives me the confidence to reach my hands round to un-hook it. I let it fall slowly down my arms.

I gulp, the nerves creeping back in. He leans in, so close to my chest that I can feel his breath against my nipple before he plants a gentle kiss on one. I lose my breath, a strangled groan erupting from my throat. Thankfully he takes my encouragement and sucks it into his warm, wet mouth.

He takes turns between flicking his tongue over the tip

and sucking hard, so hard I'm forced to cry out. His other hand gently palms my other breast, swirling my nipple until it's a tight bud. It's so unlike anything I've felt before. Normally guys just grab them like they're trying to knead bread or something. His touch is so much more. It's sweet and intense. He must really know what he's doing. From the dampness in my knickers I'd say he's the master of seduction. If that means he's slept his way around the world, who cares.

I suddenly realise that he's treating me and I haven't even removed one item of his clothing. I press my trembling hands flat against his firm chest. God, he's solid, hard muscles flexing beneath my fingers. I really need to see this. I take the hem of his t-shirt and attempt to pull it over just like he had mine. Only it gets a bit stuck. Of course it does, this is *me* trying to be sexy.

He releases my nipple with a pop, grinning at my pathetic attempt. I smile shyly, hoping to God he'll take over. He removes my hands, but not before planting a quick kiss on my palms. Then he pulls it over his head and throws it in the back.

I look down at his chest. Holy. Fuck.

He's bloody beautiful. Stunning. His shoulders are broad, his collarbone muscles only adding to the shape. I want to lick him right there. He has the smallest bit of dark chest hair among perfect dark pink nipples. I've never appreciated nipples on a man before, but I can't help myself, his are perfect.

His torso is slim but sculpted and he has abs and that magic V down to below his jeans, but he's not so ripped that he's like one of those body builder types. And his arms. *My God,* those arms. His triceps are to die for, little green veins protruding from his skin. I run my finger tip down one, making him shiver. I place both my palms over his chest, feeling the heat emanating from him.

"You're beautiful," I whisper before I realise how dumb that must sound.

He smiles shyly. "So are you." He pulls my face down so his lips lock again with mine. It's the perfect kind of reassurance that I need.

My hands find the button on his jeans. With shaking hands I undo it and drag the zipper down. The minute I pull them open his dick springs free, hitting his stomach. Wow. I was right. He's big. Maybe too big.

"Don't look so horrified," he jokes, tucking some hair behind my ear. "We don't have to do this if you don't want to."

God, he's sweet. Sweet and hot. The two never normally go together.

I smile shyly. "I do want to."

I climb off him and move, not so gracefully, to the back seat. His excited eyes follow me and within a second he's climbed back too. Thank God he seems to find my awkwardness sexy.

He starts kissing down my stomach as his fingers un-button my jeans. He sits back and yanks them off me before I have a chance to be shy. Then he's on top of me, leaning on his forearms, kissing my neck all the way up to my ear. One of his hands travels down my body, hooking his thumb in the side of my knickers and tugging them down.

Feeling his hot, solid dick against my thigh is enough to have me moaning. He trails a finger over my folds as he kisses me passionately. God, I need more. Just as his tongue pushes into my mouth he pushes his finger into me. It glides in easily, embarrassingly easily really. There's no denying that I'm soaking wet for him. This near stranger. God, what am I doing?

"You're soaking," he gasps. Is he not normally used to woman dripping for him? "You're so ready for me."

I nod, kissing along his neck. It gives me the chance to

23

inhale his scent fully. Mmm. Cinnamon and... Is that orange blossom? God, it's like heaven. I could quite happily camp out in his neck for the rest of my life and not get bored.

"Wait a sec." He leans back on his heels, grabbing his jeans. He roots around in it and produces his wallet. After a second he pulls a condom out. He rips it open with his teeth. God, that's hot. He puts it on, while watching me with hungry eyes. "God, I love watching you touch yourself."

I frown, confused and look down at myself. Without even realising I've been rolling my nipple between my fingers while stroking myself down there. Woah, he's so hot I've gone and totally lost my mind. He crawls back over me, his dick nudging at my entrance. This is it. Oh my God. No going back from here.

He kisses me again, his lips so soft and reassuring. "Are you sure you want to do this?" he asks, tenderly placing some of my hair behind my ear. I hope he doesn't notice how big they are.

"I'm sure," I nod eagerly. A little too eagerly in hindsight. *Way* too eager.

He slowly glides into me, the ache down below so grateful for the contact. It's easy at first, but soon he's so deep I fear he'll tear me apart. Deep breaths, Mel. Deep breaths.

He gazes at me with what looks like adoration. He starts thrusting his hips and the pain quickly disappears to be replaced by pure, exquisite bliss. He soon finds a steady rhythm as he weaves his hands through my hair. His thumbs massage just behind my ears. It's *beyond* divine. I've never had sex like this before. I mean, yeah we're in the back of a car but I can't help but feel special. This whole thing seems special. He's not treating me like some quick fuck in the back of his car because I'm convenient. He's treating me like, well, like he genuinely cares for me. Which is crazy when you think we've only known each other less than thirty minutes and he doesn't know my name.

God, I'm having sex with someone I've known thirty minutes!! I'm a total ho bag!

I'm pushed out of my self-destructive thoughts by a hot sensation throbbing down below. It travels up my body, pumping more blood to my already overwhelmed heart. It spreads down to my toes, making them curl.

As if realising I'm close he moves one of his hands to between my legs, using the same massaging motion on my clit as he did on my ears. Jesus Christ! I'm going to come like a fucking freight train. With the already warm feeling it feels like I could burst out of my own body. I'm wound so tight I'm clutching onto his hair for dear life.

The pressure keeps building, riding me so high that I feel like I can almost touch heaven. Then I fall back down my body spasming uncontrollably, moans spilling from my mouth. I hear my own groans in the distance, as if from someone else. I vaguely hear him grunt and then his body weight collapses on top of me.

He quickly adjusts himself so I can breathe. Wowza. I'm panting like a dog.

After a few seconds of him trying to steady his breathing against my neck he pulls back his face and gazes adoringly down at me, brushing his thumb over my cheek. How can it be that I've known this man less than an hour? I feel like I've known him... Well, okay, not all my life. But for at least a week.

"It's freezing," he says, his teeth starting to chatter. "I hate to kill the romance but should we get dressed?"

Oh. I smile shyly, embarrassed that just like that it's over.

He climbs off of me, the cold turning my nipples to ice. Okay, now that it's over it *is* bloody cold. We dress silently and I can't help but feel like a dirty one night stand. How could I have been so reckless? It must be the idea of a wedding. It always makes me emotional. It's like they're made to force us singletons into re-evaluating our single pathetic lives.

The tension is thick between us and we still have to last the rest of the night here. There's no way I'll be able to sleep feeling so awkward. I have to say something. Try to break the tension. Let him know I don't expect anything from this. He's probably freaking out, thinking I'm in love with him or something.

"So...don't worry about...you know." He furrows his brow at me. I wring my hands together, trying to find a way to be clearer. "I don't expect anything is what I'm trying to say."

He leans over into the boot area, lifts the cover and pulls out an old brown checked blanket. "Stop being stupid and come here."

I'm confused. I tentatively move towards him, unsure if I've got the wrong end of the stick. He makes his intentions clear when he pulls me onto his lap. He kisses me on the end of my nose before pulling me into his neck. *Mmm happy place.*

He wraps the blanket round us so we're nice and snug. I fall asleep listening to his breathing and inhaling his sweet cinnamon scent. I just hope that when I wake in the morning this whole thing hasn't been a dream.

I wake up before him. The first thing I notice is that heavenly scent of his. And then my dribble on his t-shirt. How mortifying. I quickly and as discreetly as I can wipe it away. He stirs with my movement. Damn. This could be awkward. I hate the whole next morning thing.

"Morning," he croaks, his morning voice deep and alluring.

It gives me the confidence to look up and into his clear green eyes. It's bright out, the white of the snow only adding to the illumination. How can he look this good first thing in the morning?

"Hi," I whisper shyly.

He smirks, obviously finding my discomfort amusing. "So are you ready to trek in the snow?"

Even with his body heat and the blanket wrapped around us it's still bone chillingly cold. How the hell am I going to do this?

"Eugh," is all I can muster. Sexy Mel. *Real* sexy.

"Come on. We've got a long way to walk and the

wedding starts at three. That means we have eight hours to get there."

I nod and get my stuff together. He climbs out of the car and wades through the snow to my side. He struggles to open my door, the thick snow almost wedging it shut. Wow, it really must have come down over night. I step out and straight into shin deep white snow. My uggs are no use for this, immediately becoming damp. Why didn't I bring proper boots? Oh, because I didn't think I'd be crazy enough to be walking in it, that's why.

"Come on snow bunny," he grins. "The sooner we set off the sooner we'll arrive."

"How can you be so chipper this early? And in this situation. It's *beyond* annoying."

"I take it you're not a morning person," he laughs, wrapping the blanket around our shoulders, forcing me under his arm. Not that I'm complaining. It's quickly becoming my favourite spot.

"I need at least three cups of coffee before I'm anything close to friendly."

He chuckles causing his chest to vibrate underneath me. "You're so cute."

I'm glad he can't see me blush. We start walking, well

more like trudging, through the snow. If it wasn't for the trees arching over the road I'd have no idea where the road even is. It's strangely quiet and beautiful out here. If it wasn't so fucking 'freeze your nips off' cold I'd probably appreciate the beauty of the glittering snow shining up at us like diamonds.

"Let's talk about something," I demand, my teeth beginning to chatter. "Anything to make me not think of my toes falling off." I swear they must be blue.

"Oh, so *now* you can talk?" he grins. I shoot him an evil glare. "Okay. What's your favourite thing about snow?"

"I said anything to make my mind *off* of the snow," I groan, smiling despite trying to look angry. "But as you asked, I'd say snow angels. Me and my friends used to make them every time it snowed and then my mum would make us hot chocolate in front of the fire. It's my favourite Christmas memory."

I feel him grin next to me before unwrapping his arm from around me and pushing my shoulders back. Before I can even register what he's done I lose my balance and fall flat on my back into the snow. The ice chills my spine, winding me temporarily. Goose pimples the size of Canada shoot up and down my body as the cold bites my skin.

"Your wish is my command," he grins, deliriously happy with himself.

I stare up at him completely horrified. Does he think this is funny?

He dives down next to me, also on his back, flailing his arms and legs out by his side. "Come on then," he chuckles. "Make a snow angel."

Is he serious? But his enigmatic green eyes, alight with mischief make me want to join in on the silliness. Yeah, I don't feel like I can move from the freezing cold penetrating right through to my bones but I force my muscles to contract. My stiff muscles eventually allow some movement and I'm able to move my arms and legs. Sure it feels like lifting lead, but I manage it.

"That's it!" he laughs. "That's more like it."

He leans over me, his smell enveloping me. Suddenly I feel more hot than cold.

"You forgot to ask me what my favourite memory is," he says, his voice low and husky.

He literally takes my breath away. He leans down further planting the softest, warmest kiss on my lips. Mmmhm. I wish I could crawl into those lips and snuggle. Is that weird? Probably.

He leans back. I almost follow him, he's just so delicious.

"It's snow ball fights," he grins. He grabs my jumper roughly at the neck and throws down a ball of ice.

The frost hits my raw skin, stinging on impact. I'm so frigid with the cold I can't even react yet. Cold, cold, *so fucking cold.*

I jump up in a second, all previous stiffness gone, shaking my top so the remaining snow escapes. Fuck, that cuts like a knife. I look at him in disbelief. He has the audacity to look amused.

"H-h-h..." I can't even get my words out, my teeth are chattering so hard. "How could you? You b-b-bastard!"

I *have* to get him back. I squat down to scoop up some snow but hear crunching. I look up to see him running down the road, laughing wildly.

"You'll have to catch me first!"

That little shit.

We chase each other with snowballs until my fingers feel like they're going to drop off and my legs feel like they're made of jelly. The cold air is hurting my lungs from having to take in panicked breaths.

"Okay, I surrender," I pant, almost doubling over.

"Enough."

He grins, also out of breath. "Thank God. But hey, it passed the time right?"

"I suppose. Just cuddle me with that blanket again. I need your body heat." This cold is making me seriously angry. I must be coming across as a right bitch.

"I have a feeling you're going to be a high maintenance lover," he jokes.

Does that mean he wants me as a lover? And if so does he not want a girlfriend but just a booty call on tap? The minute we're connected again under the blanket it's like I'm home. Who cares what he says. His warm skin radiates through his coat. I close my eyes for a second drinking it in. Visions of me doing this on a lazy Sunday morning cross my mind. Only in my vision I'm also on a comfy sofa in front of a roaring fire. I don't know what I crave more, him or the warmth. Who am I kidding? Of course it's him.

A little walk later I feel him tense beside me.

"What is it?" I ask, looking up into his grave face.

"I don't believe it," he grins. He holds out his arm and points forwards.

I follow it to see a little snow covered wooden shack with only one pump in front of it. A hanging sign says 'Petrol, cash only.'

Well this looks like the kind of place you get chopped up into tiny pieces.

"We can finally call for help." He starts dragging us over towards it. "And we'll make good time." He gets his phone out of his pocket to check the time. "Shit and I've got service!"

Finally, we're back into some kind of civilization.

"Come on, lets go in and see if they have any food."

The relief makes my body sag, although I still think this looks like the start of a horror movie.

I frown. "Are you sure this place is safe?"

His face lights up in amusement. "I think we'll be okay," he says sarcastically. "But just in case, I always carry my rape whistle."

"Ha, ha bloody ha," I retort, chuckling.

He's fit *and* funny. I've really hit the jackpot with this guy. Okay, mental checklist. Have I packed any sexy underwear? Err...no. Have I shaved my entire body? Err...no. But that's okay. I mean, we've already had sex and it's not like I plan on pouncing on him the minute we get back to the hotel. I'm not that desperate. It's just...well, how long has it been since a fit as fuck guy like him showed any interest in me? I'm tempted to tie him up and drag him down the aisle myself. Only, I have a feeling that would emit some 'gagging for it' vibes. And I am *not* easy. Well, not that easy.

"Is it okay to borrow your phone? I need to ring my friend and tell her I'm okay."

"Yeah of course." He hands it over. "I'll go in and ask to use their phone while I get us some goodies."

I nod and wait for him to leave. "What are you waiting for?" I ask with a smile on my face.

He shrugs. "Nothing. I just have a feeling when I go in here things are going to change between us."

"O...kay," I smile bewildered. "Stop being weird and go call AA."

He smiles sadly before walking into the petrol station. I dial Gabriella, having known it off by heart for years.

"Hello?" she answers cautiously, obviously wondering who this strange number is calling her.

"Gabs, it's me."

"Where the fuck have you been?" she hisses, her voice changed to furious in an instant. "I thought you were dead! I've called the police *and* your mum!"

"My Mum! Oh great!" She's probably alerted the local media and set up a search party by now. The woman really needs to keep taking her Prozac.

"What the hell happened? Where are you?"

I sigh, letting what's happened to me sink in. Shit, I've been in a car crash. I've fucked an almost stranger. I might have fallen in love with him a little bit. I've had a near death experience; I should be re-evaluating my life. Not trying to work out how soon we can be back at the hotel in a steaming hot bubble bath together.

"I'm okay. I had a bit of car trouble and now I'm travelling with..." God, I don't know his name.

How could I have slept with someone whose name I don't know? What the hell has the cold done to me? I'm a total snow whore.

"Well, don't worry. You haven't missed much. Except..." she lowers her voice into a gossipy whisper I know so well. "The groom hasn't turned up yet! Can you believe it? They're telling people he just got stuck in traffic, but rumours are spreading that he's changed his mind."

"Gabs, that's terrible." Not that it wouldn't serve that snooty bitch Olivia right. Karma and all that. "You're supposed to be her friend, remember?"

"I know, I know," she says, slight remorse in her voice. "But it's pretty scandalous, don't you think?"

Our Gabs loves a good gossip. Just joining in with her

already makes me feel warmer.

"Yeah," I answer vaguely. But like I said, I can totally imagine any man having second thoughts about marrying someone like Olivia. No one will ever be able to keep her happy.

"So who are you with anyway?"

"Um...I don't really know his name to be honest," I admit awkwardly.

"Mel, you're travelling with a man whose name you don't even know?" she shrieks in outrage. "Are you fucking insane?"

"Okay, so it sounds bad, but...he's nice."

Just then he opens the door of the petrol station and waves to me. "Could you pass me my wallet from the bag?"

I nod and open it up, passing it to him as he strides over. He opens it, takes a credit card out of it and hands it back to me.

"Was that him?" she shouts down the phone. I cover the ear piece so he can't hear her as he leaves. "God, he sounds sexy."

"Yep, that was him."

Gabriella starts blabbering on about other wedding gossip, but I've already started to zone her out. Instead I notice his pink driving licence peeping out from the wallet. I discreetly pull it out, checking that he's still inside paying. I know he said no names, but surely we're beyond that now?

He's got such a gorgeous photo. It seems to have been taken a few years ago when his hair was slightly longer. His name is Aiden Dewhurst. Aiden. My Aiden. Why does that name ring a bell? I run through everyone I know in my mind. Is there a celebrity called Dewhurst? No. Is there someone at work that I've met? No. I've definitely seen this name written down somewhere before. Oh God. No. *No, no, no.*

"Gabs," I interrupt. "What did you say Olivia's husband to be's name was?"

"Husband to be? You're sounding optimistic aren't you?" she laughs. "Didn't you hear me? The man's not arrived for his own wedding day."

"Gabs, what's his name?" I shout impatiently. Aidan's finishing up paying now. He'll be back in the car any minute.

"I can't remember his first name. I've only met him once and I was really drunk on cocktails. Something Dewhurst. I remember his surname because I thought it was funny as it reminded me of condensation."

My heart stops, his name like whiplash for my heart. It's him. The man I'm fantasizing about is the bloody groom! I'm a fucking idiot!

"Dewhurst? Are you sure?"

Maybe she's made a mistake. It wouldn't be the first time. I would have thought he'd have bloody mentioned that it was *his* wedding we were on the way to. I mean, here I've been blabbering away to him, fluttering my eyelashes like a little whore and he's been laughing at me. Maybe he wanted a quick last shag before the big day. Maybe he's in there buying condoms, the bloody creep.

"Yeah, why?"

She has to be wrong. She just has to be.

"And what does he look like?"

"Oh, he's gorgeous," she gushes. "All dark brown hair and these incredible green eyes. He makes Johnny Depp look like a tramp."

Oh my God. This can't be happening. It *is* him. I'm with the groom. I've fucking slept with the groom. And I've been telling him how horrible his future wife is. I didn't sense any 'I'm about to be married' vibes coming from him, but maybe I'm just craving attention so desperately that someone only has to look at me and I'm jumping them before planning our engagement party. What an idiot I am. I feel so embarrassed. Of course he wasn't going to turn down an eager slut like me.

"Mel? Are you still there?" Gabriella asks.

Aidan opens the door and jogs towards me smiling.

"I've gotta go Gabs." I end the call before she can argue.

"I got you a present," he says, his eyes smiling. He throws a snickers bar at me and I smile despite myself. How could this perfect man be such a lying arsehole? It's true what they say, all men are dicks. That's it. First thing Monday I'm turning into a lesbian.

"Are you okay?" he asks with a frown.

"Me? Yeah of course, just peachy!" I snap, looking towards the petrol station. It suddenly seems inviting.

"Well AA are on the way. The guy says we can wait in there."

I nod and follow him inside. It's not actually that creepy in here. Cheesy Christmas music plays from a battered old CD player in the corner. I couldn't feel less Christmassy right now.

I just want to get to this wedding. Then I can punch him in the face, call AA to collect my car and go running up to Gabs. Or my room mini bar. Whichever I see first really.

"Hey look." I turn round to see him holding a sprig of plastic mistletoe. He puts it over our heads. "Shall we?"

"No," I snap. "We shant." Is shant a word? "I mean...no, we won't."

He looks at me strangely but looks away. We wait for a painful two hours. Two hours of him asking if I'm okay and me nodding my head, while avoiding looking at him. I can't believe what an idiot I've been.

As soon as the AA truck turns up, hailing his car behind, I jump into the front seat. I lean my head against the seat and close my eyes. Close them from the hurt. Block it all out. The sex, the snow and the mistletoe.

I'm woken with a warm hand on my face.

"Time to wake up," Aidan says, leaning over me.

I yawn as I stretch. I must have dozed off. I suppose a near death experience and finding out the man you just slept with is marrying someone else will do that to a person. I smile back at him but quickly cover it with a frown. I want him to know how much I hate him now.

I look out of the window to see we're here at a very snowy Marriott hotel. The place he's going to be getting married today. My heart plummets. The snow makes it look even more beautiful. He really shouldn't be touching girl's

41

faces tenderly. Idiots like me will get the wrong idea.

He gets the bags out of the boot and places them on the snow lined path.

"I can help them up to your room for you if you like."

"I'm fine thanks," I snap, avoiding his gaze. Those glorious green eyes look like they could hypnotise me.

"Okay. Well maybe we could have a quick drink or something?"

I stare back into his cocky face. He is. He's actually trying to have another last minute bunk up with me. What an absolutely shocking, shameless bastard.

"Well...I guess I'll see you later then," he smiles nervously, raking his hand through his dark hair. He should really grow it out a bit. Be a bit more like the picture. "The big day and all that."

"Yeah, see you then," I snarl scornfully, before turning on my heel and storming off. Well, as quickly as I can storm off in soaked through ugg boots, trying to wade through this thick snow.

"Wait!" he shouts, running up behind me. "What's your name?"

Ugh, probably just wants it so he can find out what room I'm in or something. Try and come up drunk later. What a creep.

"Melinda," I almost shout.

"Oh, okay. I'm Aidan."

I snort sarcastically. "I know *exactly* who you are" I say under my breath.

Then I turn and basically ice skate away from him as quickly, and with as much dignity as I can muster.

I hurriedly check in and go to my room, throwing myself face down on the bed. Why is my life so unfair? Emotion brews up in my chest and without wanting to I feel tears streaming down my cheeks. Do I seem like the kind of girl that just sleeps with grooms? Does he just think I'm some silly slut that's here to give him his last night of freedom? What a horrible man. I break open the mini bar, and not just for the peanuts.

Loud banging wakes me up. Damn, how much did I drink? I look around me to see that I'm on my hotel room floor, still fully clothed, with empty miniature bottles surrounding me. Whoops, it seems my pity party went a little overboard. The banging comes again and this time I realise it's not my head, it's the door. I scrape myself up, bottles tinkling, and trudge over to it, my head still banging regardless.

I open it up to see Gabriella dressed in a pink and purple floor length maxi dress. Her long brown hair is tied up into a bun on the top of her head and she's got a ridiculous diamante head piece that hangs over her forehead. What the hell does she think she looks like?

"What the hell?" she shouts. "You're not ready yet?"

"Huh?" I look over my crumpled clothes. I've got one sock on.

"Do you have any idea what you look like?" She's horrified.

It makes me giggle. Talk about pot calling kettle black. She looks like a wannabe Bollywood star. Only she's from Hackney. She's not amused. Hell, maybe I'm still drunk.

"First you dump me last night and now I have to find out from reception that you're actually here! If you make me late so help me God, I'll kick that skinny arse of yours! Stop standing there giggling like a drunken lunatic." She leans in a sniffs me. "Eugh. And you stink of booze."

"Late for what?" I ask groggily.

"The wedding stupid! It starts in ten minutes. You better get that smelly arse in the shower. And PRONTO!"

Within those ten minutes we manage to get me showered, cleaned up and dressed in my navy blue A line dress that I thought to take out of my suitcase from his car. Gabriella also forced me to have a strong cup of coffee to try and 'sober me up.' Whatever, I'm fine.

I'm still hastily doing my make up as we walk into the Ophelia room where the wedding is taking place. It's an old fashioned room with red and green swirly carpet but it's been decorated beautifully. White lilies fill the room. A lot of people wrongly think they mean death, which would be accurate for today. The day my obsession with the beautiful man dies. But no, they actually symbolize chastity and virtue. Something to do with Virgin Mary's purity. I snigger to myself. Who the hell does Olivia think she is? She's anything but pure.

Different sized candles are lit, making the alter almost look like a weird kind of throne. White chairs with bows are facing towards the fake altar. There's a tiny stage with a white balloon arch, also adorned with thousands of flowers that would put Elton John's weekly delivery to shame.

When we walk in I bump straight into Aidan. He's

45

dressed in a grey morning suit with a white lily stuck into his lapel.

"Hi," he says, seeming pleased to see me. The fucking cheek of him!

"Hi," I respond sheepishly. I look around for Gabriella, but she's already abandoned me to talk to some old school friends. "I've got to go."

I push past him and go straight out of the door. I thought I could do this; watch him marry someone else, but I just can't.

"Melinda!" Gabriella calls. "Where are you going?"

I roll my eyes. Of course she'd realise I was missing the minute I tried to leave.

"Oh...I'm just going to...the loo."

"But it's just starting!" she whines impatiently. "You're the worst wedding guest ever." She smiles to let me know she's only half joking.

"I'll be back in a minute, I swear."

I duck out and go into the hallway as people push past me to get seated in time. I take deep breaths just as they close the doors. I turn, looking for an escape plan, only to find Olivia walking down the hallway in a stunning lace ivory strapless dress. Wow. She looks amazing. I could never compete with her beauty. That's all guys see anyway. Beauty is only skin deep for them.

Bridesmaids in knee length dresses, the colour of cinnamon, are fussing over her, sorting her veil, reassuring her. She's snapping at them, flustered, her face turning red. God, she's a bloody monster. She should be floating on air at the idea of marrying Aidan.

I turn away from her and start walking. I can't let her see me. I can't have that smug face look at me in pity.

"Melinda?"

Crap, she's seen me. I freeze, mid power walk and turn round begrudgingly to see her looking at me with a wide smug smile on her face. I knew it.

"What's wrong Melinda? Did you need the toilet? Better you go now I suppose," she sniggers. Obviously referring to me pissing in the street.

How can Aidan be marrying this monster?

I mumble something, too embarrassed to talk and walk away towards the loos.

"That's the one I was telling you about," I hear her say to one of her bridesmaids. They all giggle like a crowd of teenagers in a playground.

Hurt radiates in my chest. Why is life so unfair? I

suppose the popular bitchy girls will always end up on top no matter how hard you try.

I look back in time to see the doors opening, the early afternoon light making her glow like an angel. Devil in disguise more like. Harps and guitars start playing the wedding march. She glides in effortlessly like an angel. Why couldn't I be graceful like that?

I run to the toilet and look at myself in the mirror. What a mess. I've got smudged mascara under my eyes and patchy foundation. I grab some tissue and wet it, attempting to blend the orange foundation, but then I stop. Why am I bothering? No-one's here to see me. No one cares about stupid old drunk me. I'm just the girl that pisses in the street. The whole weddings probably heard the story.

I walk out of the bathroom and back down the hallway. I stop outside of the door and listen in to the registrar. Within a few minutes they'll be married. He'll be gone from me forever. That's the way it's supposed to be I suppose. Maybe that's how fate is lined up. But then, maybe fate is that I was supposed to crash into that tree and he was supposed to rescue me. Maybe I'm supposed to save him from a life of misery with Olivia.

I don't know though, can I really ruin someone's

wedding?

"If anyone here knows of any reason why these two should not be joined in matrimony speak now or forever hold your peace."

It's a sign. It's a sign from God, or the fate fairies or whatever it is.

Before I can have a second to consider it I've burst the doors open. About a hundred horrified faces stare back at me. Oh my God, what have I done? This wasn't a sign from God. This was a deluded nutter thinking she could ruin someone's wedding and get away with it. And I'm drunk. I knew I was still drunk.

"I'm...Oh my God...I'm...so sorry." I stammer before turning and trying to engage my legs. Why are they choosing to freeze now? Why God, why?!

"Melinda wait!'" Aidan shouts behind me.

I turn round to see him running down the aisle. He's in front of me within two seconds.

"What did you come in for? Were you looking for me or something?" he asks shyly, scratching the back of his neck.

"Um...no...of course not!"

"She was probably trying to find a toilet," Olivia sniggers bitchily from the front.

"Shut up Olivia!" Aidan snaps, his neck tensing up with what looks like hatred.

She jumps back in shock. Wow. Maybe I should be saving him. Maybe he's looking for an excuse to get out of here.

"Come on," he encourages, placing his hand on my arm. "Tell me."

I can feel the entire crowd's eyes on me. They must be wondering who this hussy with the patchy orange foundation is.

"No, don't be silly. You're busy, you're...getting married for God's sakes!' Do NOT slur right now.

He stares back at me with the strangest look on his face. It's like confusion mixed with fear.

"Melinda, what are you talking about? Are you drunk?"

How dare he!

"I...I may be a little drunk, but that doesn't mean you're not a horrible bastard that's getting married after shagging me last night! I may be drunk, but I have some pwinciples." I clear my throat and try again. "Principles."

"No I'm not," he says looking at me as if I'm mental. "I'm not getting married."

I stare back at him confused. "But..." I trail off as my

gaze goes to Olivia. She's standing next to a man who really looks like Aidan, but a few years older.

"My *brother* is getting married."

"Oh," I gasp, going completely puce with humiliation.

I've just ruined a wedding for no valid reason at all. Gabriella is at my side in a second dragging me by the arm.

"So sorry about this Liv," she apologises to Olivia. "Come on Mel." She gives me a 'what the fuck' death glare, before dragging me towards the exit.

"Wait," Aidan says tugging on my other arm. "You were going to stop a wedding for me? You...thought that much of me?"

"Um...well..." This is embarrassing. "You're alright I suppose." I shrug my shoulder nonchalantly.

He laughs coolly, a big smile on his face.

"Well then maybe we could have a drink together in the reception." He leans in so only I can hear him. "And I can find some mistletoe again."

My cheeks heat. He likes me. He really likes me.

"But, you know...after these two have got married." He smiles as he gestures to Olivia and his brother.

"If she'll ever leave," Olivia huffs.

"Oh just shut up Olivia," Aidan shouts in my defence.

"Yeah," his brother joins in. "Just shut up for *once* in your life."

"What?" she says, completely horrified.

"Just shut up! I've spoken to you about this before. Stop putting people down all the time. I'm not going to marry you if you're going to continue to bitch and moan about other people. I'm sick of it."

Woah. Someone just grew a pair of balls. Better late than never I suppose.

"I'm sorry," she whispers quietly, obviously horrified at being shouted at on her wedding day in front of everyone.

"I better go," I whisper to Aidan, now that the entire crowd has turned their attention to the happy couple.

"Until later then," he nods with a twinkle in his eye.

"Until later."

Thank you so much for reading Sex, Snow and Mistletoe! I hope you enjoyed reading it as much as I enjoyed writing it! Please let me know what you thought by leaving me a review!

Have you checked out my **FREE** chick-lit novel, The Debt & the Doormat & the sequel The Baby & the Bride?

Check out all of my titles here

Connect with me:

Facebook or Add me as a friend

Twitter

Website

Goodreads

Lightning Source UK Ltd.
Milton Keynes UK
UKOW05f2317231016

285979UK00001B/1/P